Rani's Remarkable Day

Words by Saadia Faruqi • Illustrations by Anoosha Syed

CLARION BOOKS

An Imprint of HarperCollinsPublishers

Clarion Books is an imprint of HarperCollins Publishers.

Rani's Remarkable Day

ISBN 978-0-35-853677-2

The artist used Procreate on an iPad to create the digital illustrations for this book.
Typography by Celeste Knudsen
23 24 25 26 27 RTLO 10 9 8 7 6 5 4 3 2 1

First Edition

For Mariam, my princess —S.F.
For Princess Zayna and Prince Zaayan —A.S.

Rani the little princess was all alone. Again.

She should be used to it by now. But she wasn't. Being the only princess in the kingdom was boring,

tedious,

dull.

There was nobody to play with. (Nobody who mattered, that is.)

She went to the throne room, to
see what Mother was doing.

"Not now, darling. The
transportation minister wants
to talk about a new highway.
It will be marvelous,
            fantastic,
                        spectacular!"

She went to the royal kitchens in search of Father.

"Move out of the way, dearest. We're creating
a menu for a party this weekend.
It will be charming,
                    enchanting,
                                delightful!"

Ah, the prime minister.
Just the person Rani
wanted to see.

"Will you play with me, please?"
"Pretty, lovely, beautiful please?"

"I'm sorry, little princess. I cannot play with you today.
I have things to do, errands to run.
Important,
    life-changing,
        stupendous tasks!"

Everyone in the palace has things to do. Places to be.

Rani, too, had things to do. "Pack me a picnic, please, Prime Minister. I am going to the beach."

"I shall sit on the sand. I shall hear the waves roar. I shall survey my kingdom."

"But you're a princess.
The beach is not safe. It's
full of sand,

and sunshine,

and everyday people!"

"Nonsense. I have Baby. His drool will scare everyone away."

And so Rani, along with Prince Baby, started for the beach. Poor Prime Minister could only watch in horror.

"Don't worry, Prime
Minister! This is going to
be wonderful,
        marvelous,
            fun!"

"Come on, Baby. Time to build a sandcastle!"

But Rani wasn't so good at building sandcastles. She became **frustrated,**

aggravated,

infuriated!

When Rani looked up, she saw someone. A girl like her. This was unexpected.

"Hello," the girl said. "Don't you know how to make a sandcastle?"

Rani stuttered,
    sputtered,
        stammered.

"You think you can do better?" she
finally asked.

"I know I can," the girl replied.

"You must have the right
proportion of sand
and water."

"Hmmpf," said Rani. "I will make the biggest, best sandcastle in the history of the kingdom."

Separately, the girls fought many enemies. They were valiant,

brave,

courageous!

Baby turned out to be the worst enemy of all.

"AAAAHHH!"

"Get away, giant baby!"

Rani found that the way to battle loneliness was to take a risk,

work together,

make a friend.

Soon enough, Rani was back safe and sound.

"I had my very first perfect day.
I made a friend, and she'll be coming
over for dinner tomorrow."

It will be glorious,
          splendid,
                    remarkable!"

For the first time in her little princess life, Rani couldn't wait for tomorrow.